Alphabet

UNDER CONSTRUCTION

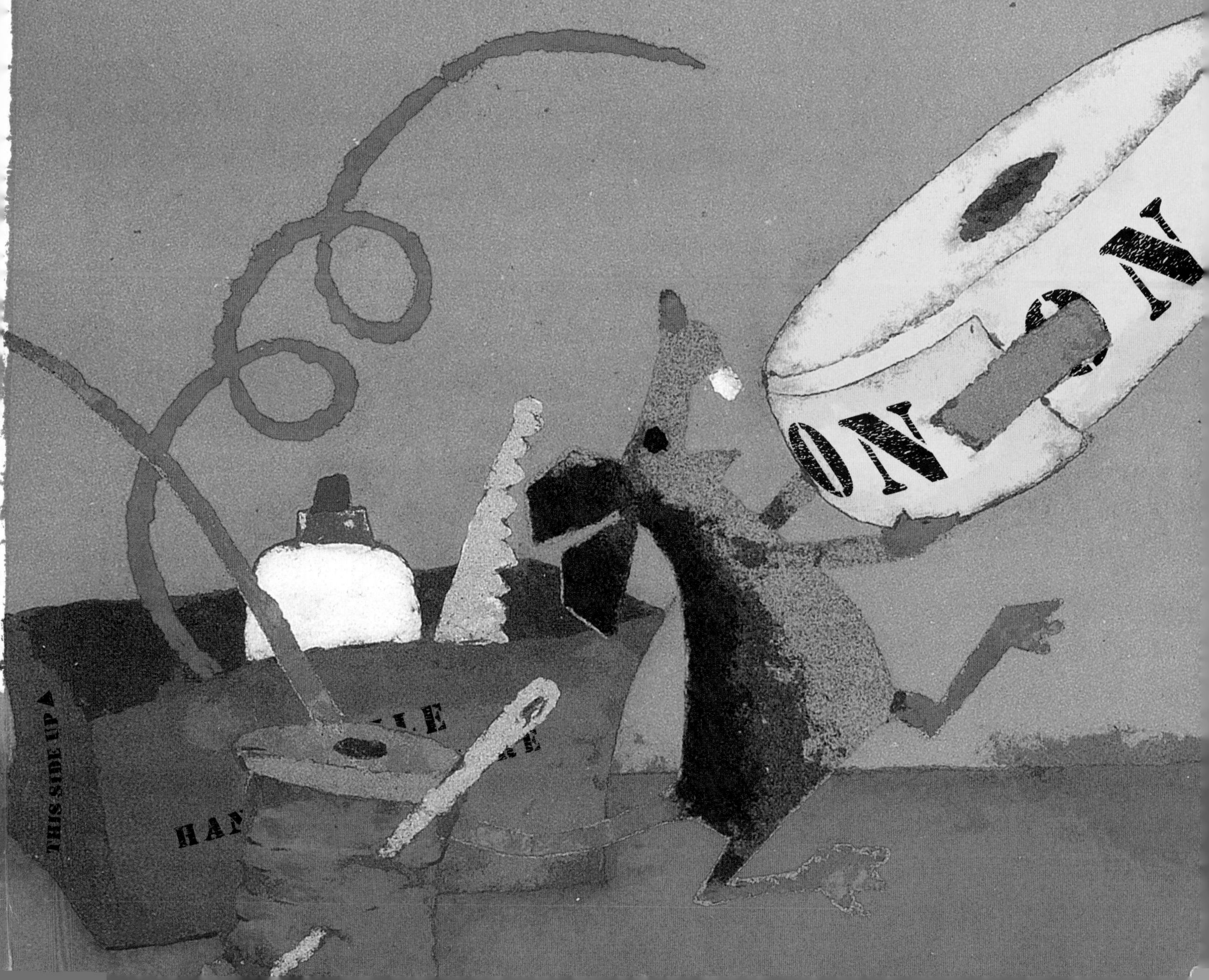

H SQUARE FISH

Imprints of Macmillan
175 Fifth Avenue,
New York, New York 10010
mackids.com

library of Congress Cataloging-in-Publication Data
Fleming, Denise.
Alphabet under construction / Denise Fleming.
Summary: A mouse works his way through the alphabet as he folds
the "F," measures the "M," and rolls the "R."
[1. Mice—Fiction. 2. Alphabet—Fiction.] I. Title.
PZ7.F5994 Al 2002   [E]—dc21   2001005210
20
ISBN 978-0-8050-6848-1 (Henry Holt hardcover)
ISBN 978-0-8050-8112-1 (Square Fish paperback)
20 19 18 17 16

Originally published in the United States
by Henry Holt and Company
First Square Fish Edition: December 2011
Square Fish logo designed by Filomena Tuosto

The illustrations were created
by pouring colored cotton fiber
through hand-cut stencils.
Book design by Denise Fleming and
David Powers. denisefleming.com

CAUTION · ION · CONSTR

Alphabet
UNDER CONSTRUCTION

Denise Fleming

For Mary Ellen,
Jan, and Linda
XXXOOO

UCTION

SQUARE FISH

HENRY HOLT AND COMPANY · NEW YORK

Mouse airbrushes the **A,**

buttons the B,

carves the C,

dyes
the D,

erases the **E**,

folds the F,

glues the G,

hangs the **H**,

ices the I,

judges the J,

kinks the K,

levels the L,

measures the **M**,

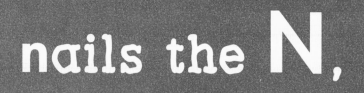

nails the **N**,

okays
the O,

prunes the P,

quilts
the Q,

rolls the R,

saws
the S,

tiles the **T**,

unrolls
the **U**,

vacuums the **V**,

welds the **W**,

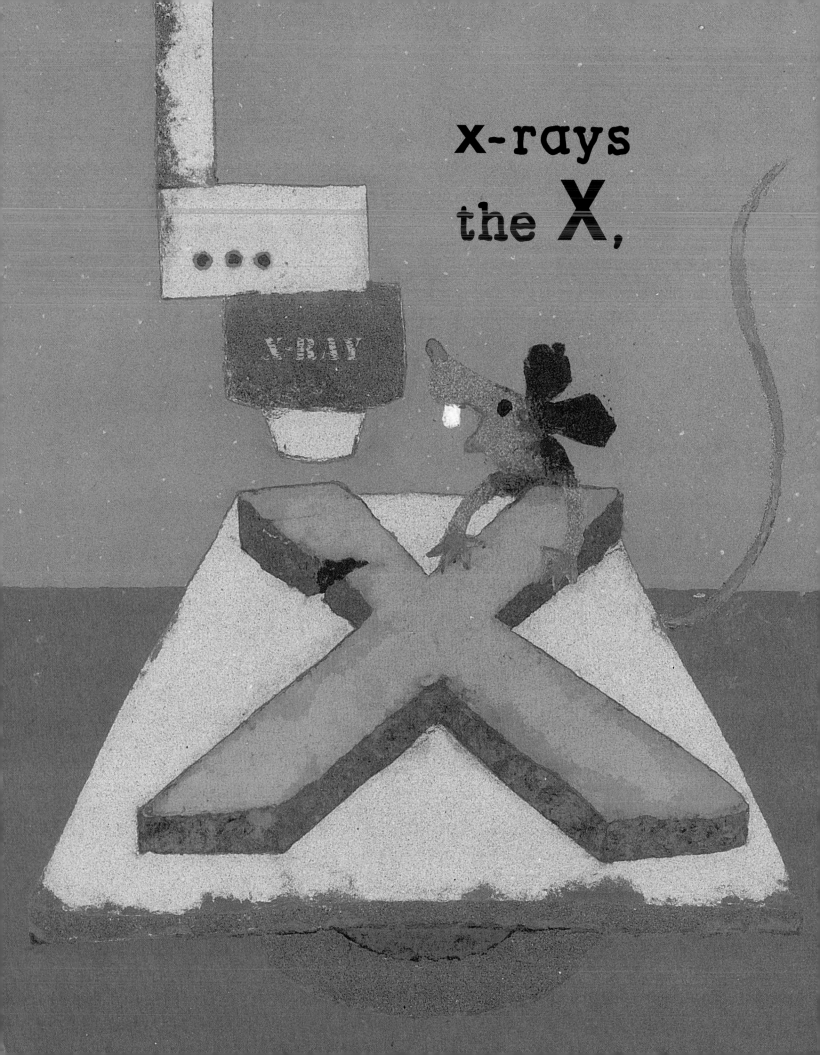

x-rays
the X,

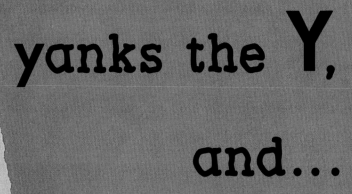

yanks the Y,
and...

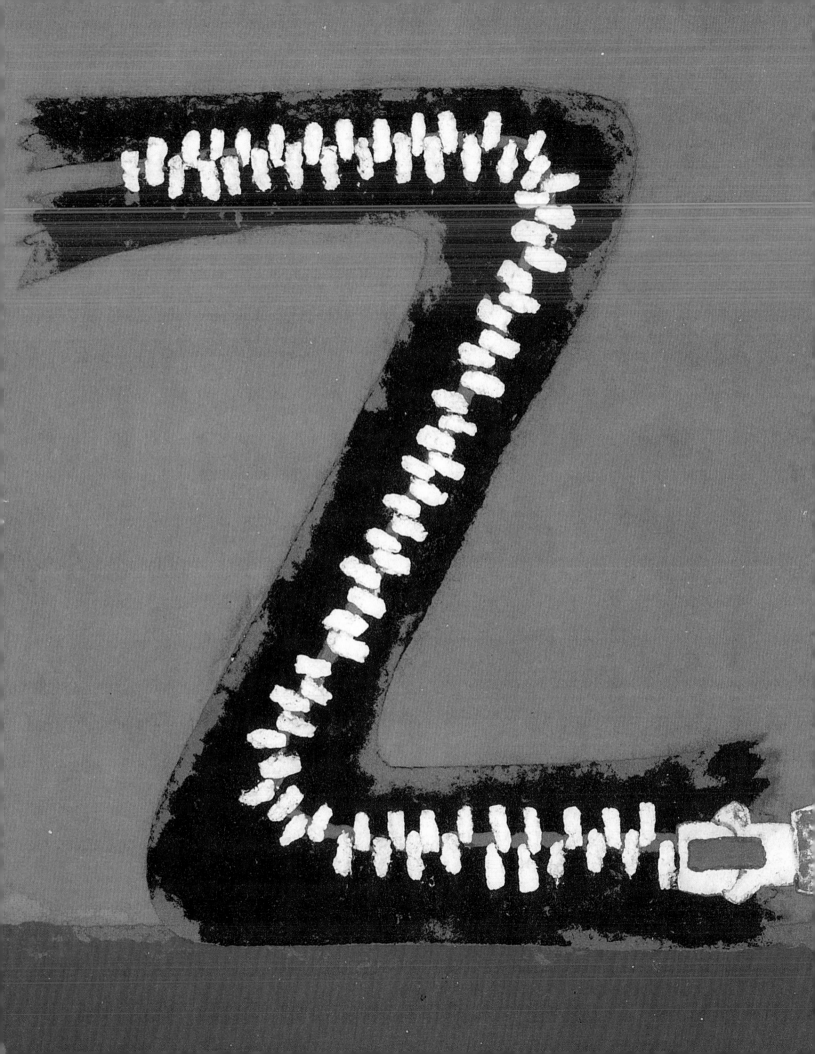

...zips the **Z**.